SHORT HAUL ENGINE

SHORT HAUL ENGINE

KAREN SOLIE

Brick Books

National Library of Canada Cataloguing in Publication Data

Solie, Karen, 1966–
    Short haul engine
Poems.
ISBN 1-894078-17-9

    1. Title

PS8587.O418S46 2001   C811'.6   C2001-900745-0
PR9199.3.S65S46 2001

We acknowledge the Canada Council for the Arts, the Government of
Canada through the Book Publishing Industry Development Program
(BPIDP), and the Ontario Arts Council for their support of our
publishing program.

Cover photographs by J. McLaughlin and Karen Solie. The author's
photo is by J. McLaughlin.

This book is set in Minion, Sabon, Frutiger and Rotis.

Design and layout by Alan Siu.

Printed and bound by Sunville Printco Inc.

Brick Books
431 Boler Road, Box 20081
London, Ontario   N6K 4G6

www.brickbooks.ca

For my parents, Howard and Hilda Solie

Contents

I Like You

Eating Dirt   13

Dry Mother   14

Signs Taken for Wonders   15

Sturgeon   16

Boyfriend's Car   17

Thief   18

Action at a Distance   19

Meteorology   21

Java Shop, Fort MacLeod   22

Days Inn   23

Drift   24

I Like You   25

In Praise of Grief   26

Three for a Friend in Lieu of Some Help   27

Hangover   30

Design Flaw   31

Other People's Houses   32

Heart Attack Song   34

Last Waltz   35

Anniversary   36

Dear Heart   37

Searching for Freud   38

Sick   39

Flashpoint   40

Night Blind

In Passing   43

Alert Bay, Labour Day   44

East Window, Victoria   45

Skid   47

Early in Winter   48

Driving Alone   49

Why I Dream of Helicopter Crashes   50

Salmon River Motel   51

In-Flight Movie   53

The Bends   54

Tenant   56

A Treatise on the Evils of
  Modern Homeopathic Medicines   57

Love Poem for a Private Dick   58

The Only Living Half Boy   60

Doll House   62

For Anne Sexton, on the Anniversary of Her Suicide   63

House Plants   64

Roger the Shrubber   65

For the Short Haul   66

Panic in Four Parts   68

Waking Up in Surgery   70

Real Life   71

Staying Awake   72

Suffield   74

Toad   75

Marine Biology   76

Ill Wind   77

72 Miles   79

Notes on the poems   81

Acknowledgements   82

Biography   83

Somewhere someone's travelling toward you,
travelling day and night.

> Anne Carson,
> "The Glove of Time by Edward Hopper."

When I got back to the streets of noises and routines,
the places full of cries of one kind or another,
the motels of experience, a fool in every room,

all the people I've been talking about were there.

> Denis Johnson, "In Palo Alto."

I Like You

"I will put it more clearly. What does
the lover of beautiful things love?"
That they become his, I replied.

Plato,
"Happiness. The Speech of
Socrates in the Symposium."

Eating Dirt

The elongated shadow suggests
my mother. To the left
a possibility of raspberries.
In the centre of the frame
I catch the sun full on
in bonnet and dainty shoes,
huge and white on the just-turned plot.
An early grinning vegetable
sprung up overnight, feeding
methodically, in fistfuls.

Greedy rhizome, I send shoots
to gorge on portions of the yard;
there I am on the step, in the lane,
under the clothesline,
and growing larger all the time.
I wonder at the wisdom
of this documentary, its complicity
in my vice, where it has led.
After all, some cravings
are only charming when you're small.

I've since learned,
when potting houseplants,
to lick my fingers
in private.

Dry Mother

Little brother, seeing
that blind wall approach,
his tricycle flipped end over end,
asks if it's the end of the world.

We who live here
in the lap of this dry mother
know from our beginnings that it will come in dust.
Have heard those drifts
that trouble the fenceline in daylight
wash around the house after dark
reminding us of how a good rain sounds
like the suck and hiss of fire.
Mornings, we've seen perennials dead
even on the lee side and have feared
the loss of each other
to shrouds of our own land spun
by wind that will not stop.

But it does this time, as before.
Another calm apology
for seed planted in door frames,
these newly-hatched sparrows
choked by earth
that leapt up to bury them.

Signs Taken for Wonders

Moments earlier we were giggling
at the new priest's Romanian accent.
"Listen to the way he says *body*,"
I said. And she faints.
My sister faints in a robin's egg dress,
sighs, leans into our mother and escapes
thick August heat itchy as cow hair
with incense, flies. She swoons.
Unlike Mrs. Stein who clattered down
like an armload of wood.

Too delicate for these dog-days,
small, clover-blonde,
my sister sews indoors.
I ask her to fashion me
into something nice, ivory silk.
I am a big girl, sunburnt
skin like raw meat, sweating
two pews in front of the Blessed Virgin.

Poor Mary, back of her plaster head
caved in, dropped in the vestry
by a Knight of Columbus.

Now mom's pale eyelids
are cabbage moths, fluttering,
hand on my sister's flushing brow.
If a sign comes today I may be
the only one standing,
strong as a horse.
Jesus's oozing stigmata, or worse,
that awful heart and its ring of thorns
jumping like a fish you'd thought was dead.

Did Mr. Schaefer receive a sign
as the tractor crushed his chest?
Doubtful. He had a Lutheran wife,
likely planting silly doomed petunias
in the clay.

Sturgeon

Jackfish and walleye circle like clouds as he strains
the silt floor of his pool, a lost lure in his lip,
Five of Diamonds, River Runt, Lazy Ike,
or a simple spoon, feeding
a slow disease of rust through his body's quiet armour.
Kin to caviar, he's an oily mudfish. Inedible.
Indelible. Ancient grunt of sea
in a warm prairie river, prehistory a third eye in his head.
He rests, and time passes as water and sand
through the long throat of him, in a hiss, as thoughts
of food. We take our guilts
to his valley and dump them in,
give him quicksilver to corrode his fins, weed killer,
gas oil mix, wrap him in poison arms.
Our bottom feeder,
sin-eater.

On an afternoon mean as a hook we hauled him
up to his nightmare of us and laughed
at his ugliness, soft sucker mouth opening,
closing on air that must have felt like ground glass,
left him to die with disdain
for what we could not consume.
And when he began to heave and thrash over yards of rock
to the water's edge and, unbelievably, in,
we couldn't hold him though we were teenaged
and bigger than everything. Could not contain
the old current he had for a mind, its pull,
and his body a muscle called river, called spawn.

Boyfriend's Car

Black Nova. Jacked up. Fast.
Rhetorical question. Naturally,
a girl would choose
the adult conspiracy
of smoked glass, darkened interiors.
Privacy. Its language
of moving parts, belts,
and unfamiliar fluids.

Hot. Mean. The words
he used for it.
She added a woman's touch.
The back seat shone
like a living skin. Oxblood.
Hair in the door handle,
white white arms
pretty against
the grain, the red.

She joined the club,
password muttered snidely
by tattletale skin.
Privacy. Bruises
smuggled like cigarettes
under her clothes.
A grown-up walk.
The responsibility not to speak
a certain silly thought.

When she asked
to go home he said
Well now that depends
on you.

Thief

Had I applied myself,
I could have stolen.
Instead, a lookout,
the easy frame, low whistle
to girlfriends manic
from nicotine, shoving
nail polish down their waistbands
in Woolworth's; chattering
dimwit accomplice to roommates
wheeling laundry detergent
out of Safeway.

Now, alone, mouth watering
for grapes, I stalk shifty-eyed
through produce. Smooth skin,
roundness, sweet green
and bitter seed will undo me
in the midst of all this pious
squeezing and ethical response
to need.

On paper, I plot
brazen daylight holdups
cleanly, efficiently, with the integrity
of someone who uses tools well.
Visualize myself moving
through aisles like a cat burglar,
ears of a safe-cracker,
sniper's eyes,

saying, out loud,
I will take this, and this,
and this.

Action at a Distance

"That one body may act upon another at a distance through a vacuum without the mediation of anything else . . . is to me so great an absurdity, that I believe no man, who has in philosophical matters a competent faculty for thinking, can ever fall into it."

– Sir Isaac Newton

Before this country of seminars,
its paranoid GNP a flat-earth theory
of love affairs, I lay
in a leafy grove of windbreak
gated by lilac, redolent,
with ants in my hair,
and considered the bodies of men, gravity
of collarbone and hip.
Amid the plushness of bees you could say
I considered you, even then hiding
from a convergence of lovers
in the pool halls of the midwest. Sometime,
I may recall a brightness to that day,
though I suppose the sky divulged
its usual kingbirds, tyrant flycatchers
jolting through standard variants of blue.
I don't believe in fate, but did then,
having already drowned the kitten
in the rainbarrel. I can't speak
to most of what you have done.

The Orphics taught when Space and Chaos,
Time's twins, first put delinquent heads together
the planet split like a watery fruit.
Fish walked blinking out of pools
on pale silk legs. Scientists still
gauge forces between sun and earth
that touch bodies simultaneously
and intimately as water.
Perhaps they can explain
the unconscious voodoo of your eye,
how that look rode north on a pilot wave

through the overbuilt world to prick me,
indolent beneath centenary ash. I woke
to an intolerable reality of Patsy Montana
yodeling for her lost cowboy
through dishcloths greying in the open window,
red-eyed leghorns pecking the yard to dust
around me, the wind-up toy of innocence
finally winding down.

I could grow plump as a finch
in branches warm as arms, believing
I had always lived
with your phantom hand around my heart.
Panic is a wire singing in air.
How can I drop my bucket
racketing down a dry well and draw love
or God like cool water, up?
We met, that's all.
If coincidence has a law
it's lonely.

Meteorology

A collision of fronts. Two thick systems
locked in downdraft forcing birds
to the ground. My knees hurt
after we talk and that kiss left me
a flower of concussion.
Heat prostration. His body
a thunderhead.
My barometer is falling;
someone, bring me a Julep. I was 30
before I realized they're bourbon.
How women of a certain age
will sit together on the porch, drink,
and watch funnel clouds pass,
breath smelling of mint.
We fucked in his car, and I will never
drive again, remembering instead
what it's like to be young,
a passenger
carried into the eye of it. Ozone
and gasoline, fern smell, rain
of hands. A nightbloomer, narcissus,
the old Ford's doors thrown wide
and a whole storm pouring in.

Java Shop, Fort MacLeod

From the highway, a signal fire on the verge of prairie
so long in half light now that it is autumn.
This is a place you know to stop moving,
the tired joy of a door where you left it
and the Oldman Valley burning orange,
all your finest summers in its leaves.
It's a hinge of worlds, for you have loved poorly now
on both sides of the foothills.

Inside, frying is a kind of weather, a Florida
for flies, the doughnuts afflicted,
the coffee malicious.
Tiny friendless salads make you weep.
You've missed him by 15 years; he rested here
travelling west one summer of his life
before you. Build him out of cigarettes,
lousy tap water, what you know of his arms
and the things he looked out on. Much of it is gone.
Lean on the past and it gives. A small grace.

When it's dark, head east
past the horse killing plant. No deer for miles.
You left a line or two in the water
farther up the valley,
though someone else lives in your house.
Cross a friend's threshold and aging passes
like an unkind word between you.
Nostalgia is a prettier season. Leaves
fall on the river and a few are the colour of wine.

Days Inn

He's not participating in the conference, no
irony in the sound of his door
closing. True fit of right angles,
metal tongue clicking home.
A neat fact and the space around it.
Then through two inches of spitboard and paint
a moment of bedsprings.
As if he has lain without removing his shoes.

Tomorrow she will perform a theory
so dense it straightens her hair.
Laptops elaborate up and down the hall.
The air is an electric fur.
Why hasn't he moved?
Everywhere, crisis in the humanities
and she is listening for the rustle
of a stranger, undressing.

She wakes to footsteps. They're heavier now,
almost clumsy. One bottle unpacked
from a paper sack thuds
a broad heel on cherry veneer.
Whisky, she guesses.
Strange off-ramp birds begin to sing.
He pours. Picks up the phone.
After awhile, sets it down.
Three times.
They could lie with hands
in each other's hair but for the wall.

At the core of all sighs is a name, a stone
from the body's last lost home.
She wonders why the weight of a man
sobbing into morning frightens her
when she has learned to travel light,
all she carries rolled tight and small.

Drift

It's been dark for hours where he's going, but here,
now, a goddamned pretty sunset. Mauve cloud
and orange light hammering a clutch
of flimsy alder branches from behind. Not much
of a tree. Last to leaf out, first to drop them,
flinching yellow in the coastal autumn winds. It's weak,
and one of these days she'll get out there with a chainsaw
and take it down.

One hot commodity, he's riding high, sweet properties
in his future. He's hitting his stride as she lies
on the couch, complex and subtle as a tripwire.
She's made some bad investments. Mutual. Ethical.
Real non-starters. Next door,
coke dealers spend afternoons on the porch,
with cellphones. Sometimes they help her
carry heavy packages from the car, sniffing.
Perhaps she's been too hard on them.
A little hasty.

For so long, every step she's taken has been toward him,
their meetings, and soon, a train wreck
of things not shared will trash up the scenery
that separates them. Don't look, he says. Best to avoid
that ugly scene, its tiresome fire.
Though smoke makes for a striking twilight.
This is the drift of them, last spike, sun sinking down.
Right foot, left foot. This is him, going.
This is her, gone.

I Like You

You name garden pests in order
to better identify the dead.
The Diazinon has taken care
of the Johnsons, you said,
coming in from the yard,
and made me a salad without
washing your hands.
It's no wonder I feel weak.
And my medicine is three days gone.
I could never keep a thing
from you. Sometimes it's better
not to speak. Your sentences
are ghastly henhouses, each word
a plank. After every lunch
I must be quarantined. But you come
and hold your hand to mine
against the glass. You are a friend,
I think, even though
my hysterical math can't discern
your sevens from your nines,
and we disagree on the function
of a denouement. You said,
only a coward reads the back page first.
Or was that me, dear,
I forget.

In Praise of Grief

Come home from a day
in the world and it talks
you down;
there's always something
you should know, some small way
you're fooling yourself.
There are people
who live whole lives coddled
as eggs.
You're blessed.

Night vision glasses, articulate
nurse, it lays
barbiturate fingers on your brow,
undresses you slowly
and stays,
holds your hand until
you sleep, mouth watering.
It's that sweet, nesting
in the cairn of your chest. In fact,
a kind of beauty, showing
what is not in everything
that is; and all
it wants to talk about
is you.

Three for a Friend in Lieu of Some Help

1

Gone is the name of muscles
along your spine, your hanging arms,
throat's hollow the hole at the centre
of that word.

When you substitute his name
for *love* it is to hold him
in your mouth awhile,
dissolving like a pill.

My face assaults
because it is not his.

How often will you say *grief*
before the sinking of that stone
is complete, its gravity,
at last, rest?

You have set yourself to this work
of mourning, are breathless
as if it were travel.

On the edge of your ruined bed
my weight restrains what wants only
to go home.

2

I would live to be
the kick in your perfect ass,
to see you shoeless and without sleeves
again in September, an autumn of men
falling around you.

Or a dog in your garden
if only to see you run
toward me, flesh of your legs
and freckled arms moist with heat
swelling corn and tomatoes
slowly to their sweet end.

Beautiful girl, come outside
or I will sit on your steps all night.
The river is thickening with frost.
Wine begs to be warmed
by your hand.

All our friends are downtown.
One remembers you shelling peas
with your skirts pulled above your knees
and hanging between them
in soft folds. How your thumb
slid along damp pods coaxing
each small fruit away.
How he walked home
with that ripeness on his tongue.

3

The room smells bad. Drowned skin.
Smeared sheets. Your children
have emptied themselves into the street
and wander the house like cats.
Their father is tired.
He has heard you whisper another man's name
and can't breathe the air
in his own house.

Today he gave me a picture
your youngest drew when asked at school
what does your mommy like to do?
You lay, looking stiff and sore
under a childish sun, tears big as your hands
and bright bright blue.

They need help, but I'm already aging
fast enough. My house plants are dying.
I haven't been to the bar in weeks
and want to talk about baseball, hear
another bad version of *Hello Walls*

with its faded man, its room
like the head of a broken clock.
His lover has taken away the soft minutes
of her body and he has forgotten
how to move in any other signature.
Weeks pass before he sees the shadow
that once pooled in her shoes
crawl, tooth-in-gear, across the floor.
The cheap watch inside him
clicks. One second.
Two.
What to do but pick up his guitar
and sing?

Hangover

Yesterday left wanting, night fell
a blank. I edged toward you
at the old hotel bar
padded in disaster movie extras
going down with their ships.
The brain floods easily,
that old engine. Later
is a lullaby of rain scraping paint
from the streets. Show me again
how to take you home.

I have a mouth full of gasoline.
What was I saying? Something.
about birds needling through trees,
the year's first wasps drilling
in the eaves. Last night,
as plants poisoned the air
under the moon, I sold you
a possibility of days on the Oregon coast
perfect as swift eggs, insinuated
Tennessee in a wet reverb,
Nashville slapback, read your palm
tracing fragrant mesquite trails
arching into purple arroyos
of the Sangre de Cristos.

Now, the day is explicit.
Swallows fall in shrieks,
from great heights. My head
is a drawer full of spoons.
No Faulkner heroine this afternoon
with flowered housedress, bourbon,
no Southern belle. My accent
makes Lutheran hymns
from what we've said of spring.
Its drug-white sea and sky, horizon
briefly gone, rethought,
and the wind full of blooms.

Design Flaw

The city settles into its grid and gears,
repeats through a mouthful of wheels the distance
from my house to yours. Between them,
men and women are trying to be happy
and it's working, a beautiful machine of a day,
bees idling smoothly in the plums and children steered
along the seawall, sun a sound motor.
I lie on my back like a wrench, like the wrong tool
for the job or an error in judgment,
considering our contraption, its constant backfiring
and exposed wires. The bad shocks.
Tricky choke. Our wild rides
among heat and oils of internal combustion.
The volatility of bones.

Other People's Houses

Other people's houses are bordered with geraniums.
Inside, bodies curve parenthetically
around all they own: a chair purchased
at the baby's birth worn to the shape it took
to soothe him, a mutual taste for Nabokov, or here,
souvenirs of a summer drive
down the California coastline, of dancing
like teenagers in one humid San Diego bar,
a blue Mercury parked at the edge of the continent
enough to stake a life upon.

These things gather the world in, close,
the way, at night, porchlights
draw lawns tightly around their homes, coats
buttoned with mauve hydrangeas.

To move into such intimacy,
to grow accustomed to the rhythmic mechanics of dwelling
as children who sleep in basement rooms,
might teach what it means to remember a body
with something other than language. That near miss,
trying always to cast bones out of words.

I'm not up to it; merely a woman
of questionable substance, say,
of low resolution, low resolve. On the streets,
in the cafés, I look just like a pile of clothes.

How simple this slide
into the indefinite, how artless.

I could tell of one spring in Saskatchewan
when sudden orioles bathed
our grain-doped eyes in orange, made nests
of strange new song in our ears, how we'll speak

forever of that season as the time the orioles came.
Or of Thanksgiving and the sandhill cranes
that spread their rippling calls like water
over fields loose with age, that bring
the crisp fruit of autumn air down from the north
and with it, months of rest.

But I've never been to Saskatchewan
and don't care much for birds. It's much simpler
when all you know about me
is that I lie.

Heart Attack Song

I have such love I break you
in my inelegant hand, a chick
in the hand of a child awkward
with love, wanting only
to be near that small life awhile.
You are so beautiful in dying
antelope fall to their knees
for you. I touch my forehead
to yours and together we see
broad backs of horses
steaming in winter, lake trout
the colour of evening clouds.
Stands of clover, alfalfa and brome,
wheatfields cross your widening eye.
How lovely, this loosening.
You shall have meadowlarks.
Parents sweetening loam
where you will lie darling
between artesian currents
and goose-bound prairie sky.

Last Waltz

Shot through
with a long Montana curve
of white crosses we drop,

clay pigeons from an amphetamine sky,
hit the Poodle Dog Lounge at twilight,
beer warm and green as grass.

The owner compensates for happy hour
by hating us, his coke-fed moon face
oscillating like a fan

as our bar tabs lengthen into parables
and the sun, overcome, lurches to the west,
the day a blue ruin.

I'm tired of this, you say,
meaning me. I catch your eye as would
a strange floater in a weedy derelict lake.

For weeks you have been gazing
down the snow-eater's green throat
to the clean young skin of a Pacific city,

in your sleep whispering
the names of grocery stores
that might provide perfect boxes

for the plates while I ride
the bed like a barge into the afternoon,
cursing your adulterous list of things to do,

your deliberate hand in its rings
writing all the ways you can think of
to tell me to take care.

Anniversary

It was the summer some rank fever weed
sunk her bitch hooks in, sowed my skin
to itch and ooze, that we shared a bed
for the first time. It's not so bad,
you said, looking for a clean place
to put your hands while I stuck to the sheets
and stunk up the room with creams
and salves. You didn't cringe,
(though in those days my back was often turned)
took your showers at the usual time, rose,
a bank of muscled cloud above
my poisoned field, and blew cool
across the mess. I said, eyes shining
with antihistamines, that you were potent
as a rare bird sighting, twenty on the sidewalk,
straight flush. It was only falling
into sleep that your body twitched away
from mine, a little more each time
I'd scratch, and I knew then we were made
for each other, that you lie as well as me,
my faithful drug, my perfect match.

Dear Heart

Rustbucket, little four-popper.
I've seen more of the surface on Mars

than of you, ultrasound shadow.
How you lay me low! Size of a fist

and the rest of me a fat glass jaw.

I get reports through the wire of veins.
Your rabbit punches, feints and jabs. I log

each personal best and sleep
like a swan with an ear to my chest.

You are the first thing I ever built,

drafty and cold despite blood's small suns.
Your joinery came out wrong.

Sweetmeat, my ugly hero, the fault
is mine. I recline and recline.

Now there is no time but yours.
What leisure you afford, what luxury.

Searching for Freud

He's here somewhere.
Everytime I want him he disappears
to the back of the bookshelf, melancholic
with transference love.
I'll bet right now he's squirming happily
under Dostoevsky.
Maybe even Lawrence.
Or Mailer.

In my dream he's two feet tall
and me, a knockout at an even six,
buff and cruel, polymorphously perverse.
You could say
I rub him entirely the wrong way.

What do women want?

I ruffle his hair, being the only one
who can reach the doorknob.

Sick

Thinking I am out of town,
friends steal my newspapers as I dissolve
like a lozenge in my semi-detached,
not quite myself,
and this starting to make a lot of sense. Outside,
weedy alders bow to weather, sighing,
wishing themselves hardwood
or southern Devil's Claw. Sullen crows
mimic wreckage and rust
and the neighbour's dog sobs with loneliness.
How solitary each noise in its net
of air, enough empty
between them for wind to bawl through
with its vowels end to end. Aching,
at least, is quiet.
The rest won't shut up. Bursting
through stalks of the mongrel houseplant
with awful furred leaves, flowers
like small red alarms
and the cat, drinking,
sounds like going over Niagara Falls in a barrel.
Curled beside me for hours, he shows his teeth
to what never sleeps in his head. You left
on the third straight day of rain, left me
the germ of an idea,
a little something to chew on as citizens hammer
the accidents of their lives into suburbs
and this first winter storm
tows months heavy and grey as freighter
and fog behind it.

Flashpoint

You need not lay your hand on my brow. I'm cucumber cool, a
temperate zone dressed for success in this tourist town rising like a
scone from the Pacific. If clothes make the girl, they make the boys cry
out for a heart ringed in Valentine lace. I have hundreds, will drop one
in your mail. But first you must take me out to dinner, as is done; for
what's paradise without protocol? Wolves in the undergrowth and no
cellphones. No background checks. Everything flowing over, under,
through, hothouses smashed and marzipan pollen settling down,
windbreak gone to seed, obscene. A regrettable dream when it
unbuttons you, stranded in a queue forgetful of the codes that make
you real. May I confess? There was one, to whom I was not duly
introduced, who laid the voodoo of his sweat on me. Our vapours
locked in a whisky cloud and Oh I Was a Drinker Then and drank
it in, sweet slick and spark, the arc that disappeared us in a flash of
heat and fossil fuels. And with eyes fixed on his pilot light burning in
another's arms a mile up the coast, I kept my oils running high, body
a heap of greasy rags. I've 12-stepped it back, thin and crisp as a wafer.
Your portfolio seems in order. A man of wire, gait clean and electric.
No hidden combustible depths or guilty secrets stashed like paint cans.
Transparent as sunlight, wind, fresh water through turbines, you know
to keep moving, how resting in love's fever of sugary leaves ferments a
dark and elemental pool that ignites will to wanting. How some suckers
waste a lifetime planted there, grinding their teeth like matches, just
waiting to catch fire.

Night Blind

Never has your Buick
found this forward a gear.

Richard Hugo,
"Driving Montana."

In Passing

Night blind through Rogers Pass,
engine popping like a rabbit gun
after an ambush of tunnels,
I brake for tinfoil, bottles,
dead stares of twisted deer.
This moon-shot boneyard
is a seam of eyes.
Immigrant rail crews lost
to the slides of March
a century ago. Two Japanese dug out
clasped in each other's arms,
a Norwegian frozen in the act
of filling his pipe. No time
even to bruise.
Hidamo. Wafilsewki. Mitsumi. Sodiatis. Sanquist.
Bronze and marble statues
for the meat ride to Glacier Station.
And the whores who died cold,
full of holes, in clapboard Columbia
or the pockmarked skin village
of Golden. A drunken doctor drowned
in a puddle of horse piss.
Years later, slide shooters
and dozers shoved 92 miles of highway
through the Selkirks' seismic muscle,
and now my four seizing cylinders
whine for a tail wind
to Saskatchewan. *I Go All The Way,*
Number One croons
over archival mutterings caught
in the black throat of the old Connaught Tunnel
buried at the Summit. Accordian ballads
of accidents that wait to happen
in the rock face, snow
fall, concentrated gravity of the gorge.
My odometer books odds of sleep
in hands and head. The cat knows it,
moving through luggage in the back seat,
throwing sparks.

Alert Bay, Labour Day

Rusted boats – *Stella Lynn, Pacific Lady* –
photograph well on black water,
their holds filled with rocks.
The men add one each night
and yell for storms. Happy hour
stumbles in from the dock
at noon, smelling of fish –
or fish-shaped memory,
since the fish are gone.
Tourists ask if the halibut is fresh.
The waitress has a bruise
on her cheek. Walls here
are made of luck and girls
walk into them.

East Window, Victoria

"I wish I had a river I could skate away on."
 – Joni Mitchell

Everything about the place
demands affection.
Sea lions roll their warm oils
like barrels through the waves, and even gulls,
from a distance,
are whitecaps flying from the garbage
of their secondary world.
So much evergreen. So much
is constant.

In Edmonton, they are cursing
ancestors and old Volkswagens, shovelling
themselves into cardiac events.
In Churchill,
snow is an animal.

Go ahead and think of May,
how the South Saskatchewan rises
muddy as a vein to the surface of summer.
Of pulling crested wheat to suck
that quick season out
through the long thick heart of it. The year
poplar and sage held you in their sunset
as you fell, leaning into a world
that did not move away.

But how dare you long
for those first mornings of frost
you bit into like an apple, the winters
skating an unbroken line
around your small clean body.
Ungrateful.

Have you forgotten about block heaters?
Power failures?
You are lost in the down time of blizzards
as thin rains fall upon the coast
and a face that you love
moves behind the warm window of Vancouver Island
looking more and more
like Mile Zero.

Skid

Black ice squats hairless
on the single-lane, teeth
all knocked out.
Molecules still
as little hands in its lap,
it hums a tune called
faster.

You asked for this,
a moonless night and snow
for Christmas. You
and your gun control,
your precious profligate antelope,
each pair of eyes a swerve. You
and your cheap all-seasons.

Black ice lays low,
laughs off the social work
of salt and sand.
One more for the road,
it chuckles, spreading. *Come on,*
you can pass this guy.

Early in Winter

The roads are bad and you miss
your old car, an even-tempered '68 Volvo,
those times jerry-rigged cardboard gaskets
and pantyhose fanbelts got you home
through worse weather, the expansiveness
of that gesture. The year's first snow

fell at noon and stuck, a thin light resting
on the firs that drags out the fade
of 4 o'clock and throws a clean sheet
over roadkill, a small blessing of dying
in winter. There is a loveliness to inadequacy
so simply put. I place a hand on your arm,

heavy clothes a door to the warm kitchen
of your body. You are deep inside the driving,
leaving me to consider the beautiful stall
of water frozen in the act of falling
from its pious glacier, to my resolve
to find an opening in this season,
feet cold, heart wagging its little tail.

Driving Alone

You learn the names given to light,
the visual heft
of a boreal forest at noon, or evening
performing by heart its declension
above the flatlands,
at the expense of your own
small word for yourself: a fence
that needs mending.
The unreadable sign. In the language
of local economies you are table 12,
room 105. Pure transaction.
A sure thing of money changing hands.

At night, scenery and time are nouns
you drive through,
double lane anodyne of wind and tires,
unable to lift your eyes from road to stars
as might a passenger
who in describing their patterns
would offer adjectives like a hand
around yours in the dark.
How beautiful. Yes.
A way of naming everything at once,
this memory made in a marriage
between you.

Why I Dream of Helicopter Crashes

At first there is only the magnificence
of rising
straight up, roaring
through a thin indifferent element.
Clothes outgrown, tiny shoes fall
away as the body arrays itself
in faith among the clouds. But soon,

that first engine stutter lifts a hand
to collarbone. In concussive measures
of the blade the chance
of a guttering pause.
Fibrillation.
Our ridiculous carriers tilt and plunge

in the casual way of machines, the eye
a window to ground
that will not let go. Movements
of each pilot's arm look much like
our own, panic the soft spot
we are all born to.

Salmon River Motel

Between dry eyes of the Shuswap
a dog-day migraine pounds as high pressure goads air
into something it can't take back,
some criminal friction with sun. Neither gives,
chest to swelling chest, lording it
as the Houseboat Capital of Canada squirms and sours.
A mountain south of the Number 1
begins to burn. Nothing to do with me.
Driving west, merely night blind, I take a room
as evening starts to run its phantom deer across the road.

This is how I remember desire:
all heat and bad timing. Red sinking sun,
brief period of blindness. The panicky swerve
from nothing to nowhere
that takes your face in its hands and screams it's time
to shut the engine down.

Hell has gone guerilla in the hills,
slipping its threats under doors. I've run out of towels.
My air conditioner is cranked and coughing.
There's a small fridge for beer.
Across the street at A-1 Taxidermy two men work
to spare their dead a decent burial of fire.
Lions lie with lambs in the rusted box of a half-ton,
a furry *Guernica*.
I watch this on TV, having removed my shoes.
Only reporters are happy, changing and changing their shirts.

The town is evacuating, air thick with the terror of elk,
and I'm thinking of a man pushing a mower endlessly
along the perimeter of a seaside lawn,
how he filled my lungs with something heavier than breath.
Of the woman who calls him in to supper.
Does this make me a villain?
If I can't sleep then no one here will sleep.
It's important to stay in character. Meanwhile,

firefighters converge as though more noble aspects
could be differentiated and made flesh.
They consume food and sleep with a purity learned
from how fire takes unto itself the perfumes
of a forest's private lives and spirals with them
in rapture above the canopy. Tending backburn,
their bodies are as fervent
doing exactly what they should and where.
Finding those hot spots. Digging them out.
It's easy to forget they are paid.

Tomorrow I'll make a run
up the corporate limit's eastern slope above
the lake hanging cold arms helpless as a bruise,
radio advising those who must leave animals
to free them, that they will gather
on the shore and be saved.
Something to tell the children.
Fiddling the dial, water bombers no bigger than flies,
I'll be gunning for the salt heart of the Island, absolved
by virtue of passing through.

In-Flight Movie

Above, blue darkens as it thins to an airlessness wheeling
with sparkling American junk
and magnetic brains of astronauts. We are flung
across our seats like pelts.

Some of us are eating small sandwiches.
Some of us have taken pills and are swallowing
glass after glass of gin.

We were never intended to view the curve of the earth

so they give us televisions, a film
about a man and his daughter who teach a flock
of Canada geese to fly.

Wind shear hates the sky and everything in it,
slices at right angles across the grain of currents
like a cross-cut saw.

Fog loves surprises.

We have fuel, fire, Starbuck's coffee, finite
possibilities of machinery. A pilot with human hands
and nothing for us to do, turbulence being to air
what hope is to breathing.
A property.

Far below, a light comes on in the kitchen of a farmyard
turning with its piece of the world into shadow.
Someone can't sleep

as engine noise falls around the house like snow, vapour trails
pulled apart by frontal systems locked overhead
since high school. Imagines
alien weathers that unfurl in time zones
beyond the horizon.

The Bends
for Nicole

"Words are inadequate to describe the peaceful solitude of inner space
  one feels underwater."
    – Dennis K. Graver

I was getting used to dark water,
insulated, extending my hand
toward everything I saw, somnambulent
fish whispering
through my weedy hair,

>   *we love what is lost to us*
>   *as we are lost to you and loved,*

when it all ran out. Time. Breath.
The boat crew left me at the bottom,
returned to their wives, toasting
my good health as they swung toward shore.

Not inexperienced, I have been taught
the safety of a slow ascent, how much pressure
can be borne by a body in over its head.
Avoid panic. The secret of long life.
We might as well try to talk ourselves
into love, be patient,
expect the worst when the worst
is always the unexpected.

I pushed off from the tilting floor
with both feet, buoyed by lungs grown large
and wild, my heart, meek cousin,
beside them. Though I knew the risks
of open air, the strange desire
to empty ourselves, unprepared,
in a brief anemone to the light,

I forgot about the pain. How blood commits
its salts to the companionable sway
of dreams, to quiet faces
of creatures who swim there, and resists
rising, thinned, to the glittering surface
of another day. Its clothing and keys,
all the reasons
we are so often desperate upon awaking.

Tenant

When the body of an animal
is occupied by a hunter lost
in a killing cold,
steam rises as souls do
from that small red room.
Such meetings are not fate,
though there is almost always blood.
Barely a coincidence of weather, weapons.
A sudden sound, shift in direction.
Movement by degree to the east.

Stop for coffee, change your life.
Embraces are crucial, but so
is the pause you make on the steps
before leaving, and whether or not
you have driven. Like trees, without intent,
we keep track of the deaths
that deliver us. Each midnight move.
Nothing vanishes. Everywhere,
scoring, scar, lovely cast of fern.

It's not surprising,
sleeping with windows open, to wake
and find everything taken.

Although there is comfort here
in the odd ceremony of ruins,
there is almost always blood.
Prying up floorboards
scraping a last reserve of coins,
my map of fastest routes out of town,
I find only a poem
of useless telephone numbers.
Your presence is the threat of seasons.
What I need to get going.

A Treatise on the Evils of
Modern Homeopathic Medicines

"What if the vitamin makes my body stop making its own vitamins?"
  – Mark Anthony Jarman

"...homeopathy is based on the theory that 'like cures like'."
  – *Oxford English Reference Dictionary*

Take four Tylenol with that last sweet shot.
Morning comes, you'll be a prince
on the phones, greasing wheels, making it go
with a clear head. Your guts will come around.
Little quinine at coffee. Cuts the shakes.
Sudden liver failure? Forget about it.
Cellphone tumours? Bullshit.
Look at me. 40 years and still a whip,
slick, the ticket, hyperspace.
I smoked my first cigarette at nine.
You don't know who to trust? Then don't.
Trust technology. It wouldn't send
machinery to Mars then seed
your little brain to polyps, plant
cancer mushrooms in your balls.
It can keep your dick hard all night.
What more do you need? Someone tries
to sell you blue-green algae. Fuck him.
It's a scheme. Vitamin C? Eat an orange
for Chrissakes. Send that joker back
to the co-op, to his hypocrite cronies
drumming in the woods reading Bly by night,
Rand by day. That'll soften your brain
fast as any happy hour. Do you think
no one is making money from this?
That it comes from the goodness of a heart?
Nothing comes from the goodness of a heart.
Like God said on the seventh day, kicking back,
feeling fine. Pick your poison
children, leave me mine.

Love Poem for a Private Dick

for Robert Mitchum, RIP

Sucker punch, true romance.
15 years I've read your name
on the door, filed my nails down hard,
managed a parade of dames
whose rich husbands tire easily,
who pull Houdinis south
with proceeds of a double cross
leaving you with only style left to burn.
A currency of pain. Poor thing.
Eyes of a neglected pet
above the glass.
Who possibly can understand
what martyrs do when falling for it.

Things have gone too far for you
to admit the boredom of waking
again to stupid noises of thirst,
the dullness of a room,
a sink, a walk downtown,
the effort to reclaim
from pretty flush of evening light
a more complex drama of sunset
glaring then bloody then black.
Remembering Mickey's, the White Orchid,
pinballing cops and thugs, your name
a bad itch in a good suit.
You kept them coming back to scratch.
Now they snap their fingers in your face.
You track teenage Connecticut runaways
to grimy dance-halls for a fin
when I could be snug as a fifty
against your ribs.

Your name, bone fantasy
of my common desire, an eternal walk
down the peeling hall, heartfelt
tragedy at the door, one hand

on the frame as if to test for fire inside.
What a lovely rush, lingering there
about to try the lock, on the verge,
blushing with sweet star-crossed nerve.
I've seen no pay in months, but shine
your shotgunned shoes, go out
for Ballantyne's at noon, or Cuervo
when the day is warm
and you're thinking blackly of Mazatlán.

When all is spent in plain sight
what's left?
Humiliation of the overdressed
made up to kill but always
at the wrong event.

The Only Living Half Boy

"Johnny Eck was born in Baltimore, Md. Being one of twins, having a brother
who is perfectly normal, as you can see from the picture on the back of this
brochure… His accomplishments today are unlimited. Look at the list on the
next page and compare it with any boy you know that has all the advantages of a
normal body… So ends this little brochure on the premier attraction of the
entire theatrical world – Johnny Eck, half boy."
    – promotional pamphlet

At the piano, in a rage, Johnny hammers Liszt to gravel,
opens hailclouds of Bach over his company's beds
on the third floor of the Ritz-Carlton Hotel.
Nature's Greatest Mistake has the pink of a socialite's mouth
on his cheek. A bobbing gin pigeon, she had bent
straightlegged, ass high, eyes to the flashbulbs
while the party howled. And him duly propped,
grinning like a chimp at wings of collarbone spread
from the silly hollow of her throat. He punches the keys.
Sforzando. Hands hard from walking.

He has a twin, a whole man, with legs of fat and flour.
A dumb lump of perspective in publicity shots.
The girl is with him, this brother, this unkindness
of blood who comes, pulling on his trousers, to whisper
They almost always call me Johnny,
leaning in to his meal ticket, lips twisting.

Johnny feels strong through the arms and chest, stomach flat
from 20 years of holding himself.
Whisky is forbidden, though he takes it,
time to time, for his heart.
Down the hall, his mother snores. Always,
his mother. Her adding machine, her dry fingers
in the take or on the top of his head. Nights, he wakes choking,
powder and rouge a sweet paste in his throat.
His father is in Baltimore, yellow with scotch and coughing.
At six, Johnny saw him through the keyhole
on the side of the bed, sobbing, pounding his crotch.

In their Broadway suits, New York's fabulous itch
for new distractions. He thinks of all the old scratch
in rooming houses west of the American Bus Depot.
Aging Circassians and swami mitt-readers singing
Root, Hog, or Die over broken hotplates. Of Coney Island
last gasp dime museums. Two shows an hour, 11 to 11.
Lot lice, sagging barkers. And the questions:
No, I don't have a sweetheart.
Just a small portion of the average meal ...

Johnny has never been able to pull off a *scherzo*, fingers
too calloused and thick. He reaches instead
for his glass. Tomorrow in Detroit he may sleep, or perhaps,
the next day, in Chicago. *Diminuendo, rallentando*, he pleads
to a heart unaware of its bodily home, of cities,
their giggling girls and the men who lead them away
thinking themselves very tall lovers.

Doll House

In a box near their bed
the usual junk. Photographs, letters,
diaries with broken locks.

When they fuck she slips away to nest
like a mouse in this mess,
to rehearse a life, edit and revise
scenes that do not fit. Who but she
can take her self-improvement in hand?
Afterward, only sore,
she has no memory of it.

She is his doll.
He runs a finger between her lips
and calls her that.

> It's true
> he likes her wide blue eyes.
> The way she fixes her small mouth
> and keeps it red. It flatters her
> when he says
> *that's my body,*
> *bring it back to bed.*

She smiles to think of him
positioning her arms, her head,
trying to make them stay.
And laughs out loud at the smooth place
between a doll's legs,
knowing exactly
how it got that way.

For Anne Sexton, on the Anniversary of Her Suicide

"Now it rose up – the life she could have lived."
   – Anne Carson

Slide her through the night slot. She's much better
on paper. In life, an awful racket, clattering
with pills. Her daughters in their rooms
ticked quietly as clocks. Neither they nor the men
who took her out like a subscription had weight enough
to hold her. Sex, abortions, famous dead friends,
she was all the news that's fit to print, bent
and popular as a car wreck. Anthologize her, quick.
She gave us the slip. Turned sideways
one day in Boston and was gone.

House Plants

Each morning, she lifts a cup
to her mouth, warm
in the habit of her kitchen. A fly
crawls up the wall, all eyes. Sunlight
makes its daily inventory
of her rooms.

Running hot water, she hears
the night bus headed east, new silk
of dresses that zip up the side,
but is distracted
by sucking roots of plants straining
toward the window.

Under guise of pruning, she cuts
green throats. Looks past the moat of lawn
swimming with hornets
to the shed, where a mower grins
and gasoline sleeps
in a canister round and apple-red.

Roger the Shrubber

How contemptible, the lawns.
These ridiculous plots, selfish little beds,
the alarming stupidity of pansies staring
like nasty children dressed for church.
Hadn't he counselled, precisely, against this plum?
Shards of kitschy yard ornaments
are blood clots to the brain of his mower.

Disinclined to college, he told his parents
that out *there*, he can *really* think,
gestured vaguely toward a cool chlorophyll evening,
lilac-tinted air. And has done well,
owns the truck. How long has it been?
Years.
His knees are shot.

Mornings, now, before the heat and flies
he thinks of napalm in his Spray-Pac,
of laying the lot of it to gravel and shale,
shutting the mouth of the earth
once and for all.

Slugs foul his shoes.
Ants mine for his anklebones.
Russian Olives are profane with wasps.
He's had more thorns in his head than Christ.

Christ. He can't sleep.
Has been dreaming of graveyards,
how fir roots break through casket walls
to bear bones away on a creaking arboreal flood.
Of his wife's smooth young limbs
thickening, scabbing, twisting around him.
Of the baby in his pine crib,
face covered with leaves.

For the Short Haul

Lying between flowered sheets he proposes
an exercise. Invites her to consider
space without depth. How a body can be said
to occupy a place lacking itself, other
even to nothingness. Distance
achieved outside the time
it takes to move.
It has them in stitches,
this three-legged riddle
of an expanding universe.

She offers a story of herself as a girl on the farm
staring outward from her cotton shift
to a star-furnaced sky. Her science teacher
seemed suddenly naive as a hen,
his lessons on gravity hopeful and forlorn,
the world too old and God a long way off.
She tells her lover she imagined then
the snap of a thread
      (long thread, lazy seamstress),
badgers pulled from warm burrows
through chimneys of air. Red-eyed
pullets soaring like swans . . .

It is half past the hour. He has risen
and is putting on clothes,
as always, socks first. She knows this as well
as the route home he prefers. Left
at the hospital, right at the college.
He will slow through the country club's
inevitable speed trap, turn
onto a street she has never seen. Return
to a house remote as a quasar, to a woman
who breathes into being with him
an unimaginable life.

It is February, that bleeder month
unable to sustain a normal course of days.
Spring comes too early here for anything
to find proper rest. The sea pulls itself together.

Bedding down in the trough of dark hours
she thinks it equally possible
that the infinite vaulted cathedral is collapsing,
its brainless systems sprung, banking inward,
but didn't think it worth mentioning.
None of it will happen in her lifetime.

Panic in Four Parts

I

It's nothing, really.

A sliver of glass
just under the skin.

One of many small things
that travel blood
to the heart.

II

It's not a question
of empathy. You know she fears
the slow leak that begins
a body's dispersal in death
and does not consider this easing
into cold a kindness. Forget
what you've read in *Ladies' Home Journal*.
Illness is not a pottery wheel
spinning saints from terminal clay.
Come down to it, she would prefer *you*
between those clinging sheets,
to hand off her curse of ceilings.

III

Retrovirus, misplaced gene,
ancestral monkey wrench.   Of course –
that shiftless lot
in illfitting sepia woollens.
Too long off the main road.

Few could meet the camera's eye.

Wasn't there an aunt
of 31 stone? Rumoured asylums,
extended "vacations"? A cousin
who sold a kidney for a gambling debt?
Anger morphines through her goddamning
the frayed helix turning up
like a bad penny, turning up
snake eyes.

IV

Dreams are seldom visions.
Those voices come
from down the hall and trees in darkness
are still trees. Anything
that keeps us up at night
becomes desire: a fond reminiscence
of branched lungs, fluttering
aortic arch. Radiation gossips
her body's private life. Black
tangled swells, somnambulist poppies
bloom with the natural violence
of a thing washed up on shore.
Doctor, doctor, voyageur:
her heart is a map without rivers.
Non-negotiable, secure.

Waking Up in Surgery

"But then I heard the surgeon chuckle... and I thought he wouldn't be laughing
if I was dying."
  − *Globe and Mail*, July 31, 1999.

There is no exact science to keeping you under.
An anaesthetist with an artist's soul
thinks of skating
under a high white sun among glittering birches.
Midsummer, but his instruments
are icy as December railings, your body
a landscape in wintergreen

and a doctor in up to the wrists, paring,
excising. Cutting you loose from yourself.
It takes a minimum of seven hours
to bypass the heart.
You hear every word, details
of his misfiring Jag, renovations to the cottage,

and you mortgaged to the hilt. Expressionless.
Immobilized by the curare of fear, brain
a digger wasp desperate with autumn
behind hot panes of your eyes. Mad
from the truth of time, its whine
rising to crescendo inside, sawing. Wild
to make anyone hurt this way
before it finally lies down in the leaves.

Real Life

A woman, walking in her city,
sees something beautiful.
It may not be the preludes and fugues
of harbourfront or breakwater, nor
that great blue heron who rests
year after year in the big cedar
bordering a popular park. Sometimes,
small things give themselves up to us,
or we to them: a delicate lettuce
of spearmint moss on a bus stop bench,
a length of pipe rusted in baroque filigree.
Whatever it is, seeing it, the woman
thinks that if ever there were a time
to fall on her knees, this is it;
but doesn't, seeing that it's mid-morning
and the street full of bachelors.

Staying Awake

I

It's agreed.
Fall is the time for it.
Harvest done,
insurance paid up.

This is the third in as many years
and how curiously, neighbours say,
each in his own way.

The first hung himself in the barn
seeking comfort, we suppose,
in the rising smell of hay
and warmth of his horses.

The second,
hands around wrenches in his pockets,
drowned in the dugout in back of his house
among trout stocked that spring.

But this last,
so violent.
Nothing romantic about a shotgun in the mouth.

> Young guys crowd around the truck
> towed from his yard into town.
> *Is that blood? Is it?*
> *Just dirt?*
> *Is this bone or glass?*

In time this death too becomes a cliché,
like the way his living body fit
into hollows of the land,
how his vision curved with the fenceline.

Air, water, and finally, blood.
We imagine it
crawling and soaking into earth
he'd worked since he was a boy.

II

The wives don't talk among themselves,
each believing her man's mood
a secret between them.
Those days,
sometimes a week after such a death,

they move in heavy silence with him
as quiet grain moves.
And while the empty prairie sky is filled
with clouds of its men sleeping,
each woman, unheard, hides ammunition
in jewelry boxes and underwear drawers,
her nights all the darker for being awake.

Suffield

From the base, gunplay of soldiers
practicing to erase history, to cancel
like a stamp how long it takes
to build a person, a house.
Year after year he hears this
over the whine of transports carrying
cattle and pigs to the end of time,
the moans that float behind, one red leaf
in the slipstream, and grows old
in the manner of those who live
beside the highway listening
to the engines pass, his hands
fists with a glass at the centre,
delivering rye in blows to the head and gut.
No one stops.
Anyway, his pumps are nearly dry,
while he seeps bitter
as an alkali slough, as though he had spread
his body with salt and given it up
to wind and hours. Is it fall, again?
There is clamour in the wetlands, goslings
deep in their first season of guns.
All that sits is in need of paint
and the rest goes,
everyone with more miles to the gallon,
hoping to slice a few minutes off the trip.

Toad

I am a seed, a world inside
a tough weathered wrinkling
of vegetable green.
Insoluble in liquid space
of anger, fear, love,
or other human acids,
I sit on the bottom like a stone. Shifting
only slightly with tremor
or violent wave,
I ride out the winters.

But do not mistake
the stillness of my living for cold.
I am warmed enough in my smallness,
in my wet and quiet,
so as not to be judged
by warm-blooded standards.

Invisibility is my loveliness.
In assuming the posture of water or earth
I am reclaimed, while you,
large and cold and sinking on your shores,
can only hear my voice, my beauty,
through the air.
Just listen.
Even when I cry for you
it sounds like singing.

Marine Biology

We make it the sum
of our salts and muscle, a mirror
giving us back to ourselves,
our first crush, the romance of self
poured into earth's old bowls.
How pretty we look
inlaid with green and a necklace of terns
or how sad, each love affair
another lost sailor. In tides
we discern our strength of resolve,
sonorous waves of human spirit,
that eternal relentless
media darling. Regarding ourselves
from the shore is what we do best,
pulled this way and that by the moon.
With bivalve organs shifting softly,
soul sounding
in our sexy seas and the brain
in its brine, we are innocent
as nutrients. Warm inside
our big sweaters. To return
means drowning among creatures that hate
our true grit and diesel, the way we love
what we love to death
from a desire to name what swims
inside us. The last frontier.
Cod hide behind furnitures of reef.
In places, ice is metres thick
and sturgeon in the lower rooms
reach with their gills for another era,
ancient hearts beating,
waiting us out.

Ill Wind

" ... yet this inhospitable region is inhabited by a people who are accustomed to
the life it requires."
      – Sir Alexander MacKenzie

" ... the southern part of the Saskatchewan country... has not inaptly been
termed 'desert.'"
      – Captain Thomas Blakiston, officer with John Palliser's expedition,
        characterizing the area that would come to be known as
        "The Palliser Triangle," 1859.

An early spring chinook forces itself
through the skeleton keyhole
of Palliser's desert. No evening larks.
They call this one a banker's handshake.
Count your fingers.

In the bar, temporary local help
for transient Casanova gas well outfits.
Farmers are home watching topsoil call it a day
and lift off toward Manitoba, watching roots
of nursery poplars lose their babyish grip, wishing
they could gather it all in their arms.

These men suspect *El Niño*'s unwholesome
immigrant weather, contagion from incubators
of the deep south. A few remember relief trains,
dry foreign mothers in faded Easter dresses,
cirrhotic fathers, how poverty spreads like tuberculosis.

"Another wetback crashing the border.
That's how it happens. They let the niggers march,
and now the faggots have their own parade
and you can't get to the ski hills for the Indians
blocking the roads. I tell you,
I'm glad I decided to raise my kids in a small town."

A collective nod. "Fucking rights."
One, perhaps, thinks

"I did not decide. I have not decided."
Rye strokes the back of his neck. He leans into it.

Soon, midnight, inevitable arguments
and the panic of spring howling
into the time of satellites.

Beyond the elevators, their creaking annexes,
past the slough, the dump,
far below a drifting field, bodies pressed
between leaves of a nostalgic planet
among memories of a sea, its delicate ferns
and pearly shells, revolve surely
with a world's slow weight
in peace and calm and quiet.

The men repeat themselves past three, postured
as if waiting for one of their number to be chosen.
Windows smoked, walls and ceiling painted black,
the cops can't see inside.
If there were any cops around.
Just gravel like stray bullets. A sneak
of sand. Power lines wail, barely holding.
Everything happens here, then nothing
for a long long time.

72 Miles

in memory of Ivor Solie

First week in November. A mild fall. Sandhill cranes have yet to rest in stubble fields of the Wilde Hills on their way to wintering grounds in California. The yard sleeps its ochre sleep. In his small house, a bulb burning into the plain of noon attends all he has collected, the last kindness a home offers to those who dwell alone, who broach the question of their living in silence. Mute rush of crumbs, his work clothes a husk on the floor. We think of him rising, washing, making tea, and have only the sound of wind. A rural ambulance bore him west past fragrant pastures, land at ease in fallow, crossed Alberta's threshold in morning dark and hit asphalt a half-hour from Medicine Hat, where we buy our guns and clothes. Our liquor. Our cures. The Secondary 41 is more familiar than kin to us, how it winds around ancient alkali sloughs, its fenceline climbing to the straightaway and down to where the city lies in practical repose beside the river. To where no one could stop his heart's return to itself as muscle.

When late July storms roll over the southern Sweetgrass ridge, birds turn quiet as plums. Thunder revs on electric air that drives the day's pressures before it, charging things with the animus shining behind the screen of the visible world, its mouth watering ozone breath and lightning forking from the black birthplace of funnels. Bone china rattles. There comes a time we must look away from the beauty of this gathering, this convergence of light and sound, time and space. The nothing that is everything at once. We remember strikes to the antennae on the roof, how as children we were sent to gather screws popped from the eaves and cooling in long grass as crickets crawled from under the foundation and began again to sing. Uncle. Brother. Brother-in-law. We are so few now the government has taken our doctors. It's 72 miles to town and half of these are gravel lined with sage and shotgunned signs. We pull together what we know, the contents of our own hearts' rooms so suddenly made strange to us.

Notes on the poems

The lines by Anne Carson used as an introduction to the book, and as an epigraph to "For Anne Sexton, on the Anniversary of her Suicide" on page 63, are both taken from "The Glove of Time by Edward Hopper," published in her collection *Men in the Off Hours*. New York: Alfred A. Knopf, 2000.

The introductory quote from "In Palo Alto" by Denis Johnson appears in his volume of collected and new poems, *The Throne of the Third Heaven of the Nations Millenium General Assembly*. New York: HarperCollins, 1995.

The lines from Plato that introduce the first section are taken from *Greek Philosophy: Thales to Aristotle*. 2nd ed. Reginald E. Allen, ed. New York: The Free Press, 1985.

The Sir Isaac Newton quote used as an epigraph to "Action at a Distance" on page 19 is taken from the textbook *Meteorology*. 6th ed. Richard A. Anthes, ed. New York: MacMillan, 1992.

The Richard Hugo lines that introduce the second section are from his *Selected Poems*. New York: W.W. Norton & Company, 1979.

The epigraph to "East Window, Victoria," on page 45 is from Joni Mitchell's song "River" included on her album *Blue*. Warner Brothers Records Inc., 1971.

The epigraph to "The Bends" on page 54 is taken from the manual *Scuba Diving*. Illinois: Human Kinetics Publishers, 1993.

The line by Mark Anthony Jarman used as an epigraph to "A Treatise on the Evils of Modern Homeopathic Medicines" on page 57 is from the story "Uranium City Rollers" included in his collection *19 Knives*. Toronto: Anansi, 2000.

Quotations from Sir Alexander MacKenzie and Captain Thomas Blakiston used as epigraphs to "Ill Wind" on page 77 are from *Papers Relative to the Exploration by Captain Palliser of that Portion of British North America Which Lies Between the Northern Branch of the River Saskatchewan and the Frontier of the United States; and Between the Red River and Rocky Mountains*. New York: Greenwood Press (first reprinting), 1969.

Acknowledgements

Earlier versions of some of these poems have appeared in *The Malahat Review*, *The Fiddlehead*, *The Capilano Review*, *Dandelion*, *Event*, *ARC*, *Indiana Review*, *Sub-TERRAIN*, *Prism* international, *Introductions: Poets Present Poets* (Fitzhenry & Whiteside, 2001), *Hammer and Tongs: A Smoking Lung Anthology* (Smoking Lung, 1999), *Breathing Fire: Canada's New Poets* (Harbour, 1995), and in a chapbook, *Eating Dirt*, published by Smoking Lung Press. My appreciation to the editors of each.

Many thanks to the participants, faculty, and staff of the Banff Centre for the Arts' 1999 Writing Studio, and especially to Don McKay. Thanks also to the Canada Council for the Arts for the travel grant that enabled me to attend. My deepest gratitude to my editor, Barry Dempster, for his intelligence and patience, his sniper's eye and safe-cracker's ear.

To Brad Cran and everyone involved with Smoking Lung Press. Brad's encouragement, advice, and tireless work in support of new writers has in no small way helped bring this book about, not to mention almost single-handedly revitalizing the poetry reading scene on the west coast. Cheers.

To Gary Anderson, Terri Jensen, Phil Uren, and all my friends of the Lethbridge diaspora. And to Mark Jarman, Adam Chiles, Nicole McLelland, and the good people of Thursday's bar, for sharing this thing, among others, with me.

And, as always, to my family.

Biography

Karen Solie was born in Moose Jaw and grew up on the family farm in south-west Saskatchewan. Her poetry, fiction, and non-fiction have appeared in numerous North American journals, including *The Fiddlehead, The Malahat Review, Event, Indiana Review, ARC, Other Voices,* and *The Capilano Review.* She has also had her poetry published in the anthologies *Breathing Fire* (Harbour, 1995), *Hammer and Tongs* (Smoking Lung, 1999), and *Introductions: Poets Present Poets* (Fitzhenry & Whiteside, 2001). One of her short stories was featured in *The Journey Prize Anthology 12.* She currently lives in Victoria, BC, where she teaches English.